This book belongs to :

_____

Printed in the United Kingdom by Calverts Design and Print Co-Operative on FSC® certified paper

First printing December 2020

9-10 The Oval, Cambridge Heath, London E2 9DT

https://www.calverts.coop

ISBN 978-1-8383355-0-2

ANIMAL AVENUE

TO MERRY FROM ANDREW

Story by Andrew Bradley *ME*

Illustrations by James FitzGerald

Poor Bonaparte awoke with a start.
Outside was a terrible squawking

All down the street, people jumped to their feet.

Every building was full of eyes gawking.

At Number 4, the Singhs rushed to the door.
A flamingo stared in through their window.

Dr Boto quickly took a photo
as a coyote ran off with his tea.

Giggling gibbons swung through the shutter.

Mashka and Melodie were aflutter.

Dear Granny Ginny got in a spinny.
Tropical birds were eating her herbs.

Bonaparte couldn't believe his eyes.

Animals from the floor to the skies.

People had said the zoo might close.
Now creepy crawlies lived under his nose.

The neighbours asked: "What shall we do?
Our street cannot become a zoo!"

"Why don't we adopt an animal each?
See what we can learn and what we can teach?"

Window cleaners employed the giraffe

who reached up higher than previous staff.

Garage hunks used elephants' trunks

for washing windscreens, without machines.

Humans and animals side by side.

Teamwork gave them lots of pride!

A crocodile towed boats down canals.
Monkeys delivered post to pen pals.

Ginny was having a laugh with a giraffe

as a baby hippo soaked in the bath.

Bonaparte now woke without a to-do.
His new alarm a ...

COCK-A-DOODLE-DOO!